THE
LOG CABIN
WEDDING

THE
LOG CABIN
WEDDING

by Ellen Howard

illustrated by Ronald Himler

HOLIDAY HOUSE / New York

Text copyright © 2006 by Ellen Howard
Illustrations copyright © 2006 by Ronald Himler
All Rights Reserved
Printed in the United States of America
www.holidayhouse.com
First Edition
1   3   5   7   9   10   8   6   4   2

Library of Congress Cataloging-in-Publication Data

Howard, Ellen.
Log cabin wedding / by Ellen Howard ; illustrated by Ronald Himler. — 1st ed.
p. cm.
Summary: Although it was her idea to bring together her family
and that of a neighboring widow woman to reap the harvest,
Elvirey feels her heart squeeze tight at the thought of the widow
and her Pap getting married.
ISBN-13: 978-0-8234-1989-0 (hardcover)
ISBN-10: 0-8234-1989-4 (hardcover)
[1. Remarriage—Fiction.
2. Frontier and pioneer life—Michigan—Fiction.
3. Family life—Michigan—Fiction.
4. Michigan—History—19th century—Fiction.]
I. Himler, Ronald, ill. II. Title.
PZ7.H83274 Low 2006
[Fic]—dc22
2006043399

For Mama,
who insisted I could not leave
Elvirey forever without a mother.
E. H.

Contents

THE
LOG CABIN
WEDDING

Chapter 1

Trouble

The corn was taller than my head. The wheat swayed heavy and gold.

"Harvest tomorrow, Elvirey," Pap said as we walked between the rows. There was pride in his eyes, but sadness, too. "Iffen only your mam could see this corn," he said.

"Mebbe she can." I patted his hand.

"Mebbe." He gave himself a shake. "Let's see what your sis has for supper," he said, "and if your granny's on the mend."

Granny had been poorly for some days.

We was almost to the cabin when we heard

my big brother's yell. Pap took off running. When I got there, he was kneeling over Bub, looking like thunder.

Bub was hanging onto his knee.

"What's amiss?" I called.

"He fell outen the tree," said Sis from the doorway.

Pap felt of Bub's leg with his hands. Bub hollered.

"What fool thing was you up to?" Pap cried.

"I was just a-playin'," he said. "Seein' how high I could climb."

Pap hauled him up, rough-like.

"When we start harvest tomorrow?" he said, disgust in his voice. "Don't you know you'll be needed?"

Granny lifted herself up in the bed as Pap carried Bub inside, Sis and me right behind. She looked at Pap, fuming, and Bub, weeping.

"He didn't do it a-purpose," she said. "Elvirey, wet a rag in the spring and fetch it to your brother."

I ran out quick to do as I was bid.

Behind me, I could hear Bub wail. "I'll be fine. Just leave me bide awhile."

When I came back, Sis was soothing Pap. "Elvirey and me, we can help with the harvest. Don't you fret yourself."

"I can help, Pap," I cried. "Just see iffen I can't!"

But Pap didn't look at us. He slumped on the doorstep, his head in his hands. "Better crop than ever I growed in Carolina," he mourned, "and but two bits of gals to help gather it."

"Ow-w-w!" Bub hollered when I slapped the cold poultice on his knee. But in a minute he perked up. "It's a-feelin' better already, Pap. I'll be fine tomorrow."

Pap just shook his head.

Chapter 2
Elvirey's Idee

On the morrow Bub couldn't hobble to the privy his knee had got so swole.

"Do you think it's broke?" fussed Sis.

"Just sprung," Granny said. "He'll mend. But he needs to stay offen it."

Pap snorted and pulled up his galluses. "I knowed it!" he said.

"Just put him in the bed with me," said Granny. "I'll see to him. Go harvest your dad-blamed crops."

"Who's goin' to see to *you*?" Pap said.

"Don't you fret about me," she snapped, her eyes sparking. "I've nursed *you* many a day."

All this time, Sis was emptying the slops and putting corn cakes and water nearby the bed and washing Granny's face and hands and changing the poultice on Bub's knee and tidying the bed-clothes.

I was helping.

Pap was lacing his boots.

"Come eat your breakfast, Pap," Sis said. "Come eat your breakfast, Elvirey. We got work to do."

But I was already working. I was working my brain.

"Pap," I said.

He didn't hear, my voice was so meek.

"Pap," I said louder.

"Pap!" I 'most yelled.

"Son, mind that child," said Granny.

"What?" Pap said, raising his head. "What the tarnation you want, Elvirey?"

"I got an idee," I said.

"What idee?" he said.

"We need help," I said.

"Tell me somethin' I don't know."

"Mebbe somebody else needs help." I was remembering the Widow Aiken, who had come to a meeting at our cabin.

"Somebody who?"

I told him.

He turned away, so I said to his back, quick-like, "She got boys, but no man. We got a man, but no boys."

Pap turned back. He looked at me close.

"Many hands make light work, Mam used to say," I said.

So, I reckon it was my doing, Pap and the Widow Aiken. It was my idee.

Chapter 3
The Widow Aiken

That very day, Pap made a bargain with the widow.

"It was downright pitiful," he said that evening at supper. "That poor woman and them boys've been tryin', but they've scarce begun. Them boys need a man's strong hand."

We began next day at our place.

Tobias was the biggest Aiken boy. Pap set him to scything the wheat with him. He put Lemuel to work with Sis and me, gathering the sheaves and stacking. The widow stayed at our cabin to see to Gran and Bub, which set Pap's mind to rest.

Down the rows Tobe swished, with Pap

a-hollering if he slowed or if Lem and us fell behind.

"Mind you don't get in the way of the scythes, Elvirey," Sis said, like I was a babe. I shot her my poison look, but Tobe said, "Don't you fret none, miss. I'm a-watchin' out for her."

Then he gave me a wink.

Two days later we picked the corn.

By the time it was in the crib, I could see the widow had set her snares.

We'd come in of an evening, hot and sore and weary, and there she'd be at the cabin door, with water hotted and soap laid to hand, all smiles and soft words. Granny was propped in the bed like a queen and Bub a-setting up. There was good smells of supper and the cabin so tidied it scarce looked like our'n. The table was set with a cloth and a jug of flowers.

Wildflowers, like our mam used to put in that jug.

My heart began to hurt.

If the widow said "boo," Pap jumped.

"Won't you say the blessing, Mr. Freshwater," she'd say. Pap would bow his head, meek as a lamb.

"I appreciate your guidance for my boys," she said. Pap grinned like a boy himself.

"You'll make short work of my few acres, Mr. Freshwater," she said. I believe Pap redded up!

When she and the boys'd gone home for the night, my folks couldn't cease praising her.

"My knee is 'most like new," Bub said. "She's a sure enough doctor."

"What a cook!" said Sis. "I think she's purty, too."

Pap said, "That widow woman does beat all!"

"I'm glad they've gone home," I said, kicking the table leg.

Granny looked at me sharp. She was setting up in her chair now, the color back in her face.

"This was your idee, Elvirey," she said.

So I kicked the table again!

Chapter 4
Better Than Their Ma

"I'm a-goin' with you to the widow's today," Bub said next day, limping across the cabin to show how he was healed.

"You'd be no use with that knee," said Pap. "You stay with your granny and tend to her needs."

"Aw-w-w, Pap!" Bub said. "Nursin' is women's work."

"The gals in this fam'ly been doin' your work," said Pap. "I reckon you're fit to do their'n."

Sis put her hands over her mouth. I looked at the floor, trying not to laugh. Bub looked like to chew nails.

But my heart was light. With the bargain half done, we'd soon be shut of the widow.

She and her boys was already in their field when we got to the Aiken place, Pap and Sis and me.

"You go on in now," Pap said to her, his voice all tender-like.

"Us younguns is plenty to help," I said. I hefted a sack and stomped down the row.

"Dinner's in that basket yonder," I heard her say. "There's nothing to do in the cabin 'til supper time."

So she worked alongside of him, just like a man, breaking off the ears of corn. We younguns gathered them in sacks. When mine got heavy, Lem toted it for me.

The sun rose hot. Tobe traded Sis his hat. I had to laugh to see that boy wearing a limp sunbonnet.

I liked them boys better than their ma.

The Aikens hadn't cleared as much land as us. Their harvest wouldn't take long, Pap said. He seemed right sorry.

But under my breath, I said, "Good!"

"You goin' to have enough to get you through the winter?" I heard Pap ask her.

"Reckon we'll manage," she said.

Chapter 5

Willow Pattern Plates

Late in the day, I felt a hand on my arm. It was *her*.

"Will you help me get the supper on, Elvira?" the Widow Aiken said.

But my heart was squeezed so tight I couldn't answer. *Elvira* was what my mam had called me.

"Elvirey?" said Pap.

I kicked a clod of dirt. "I reckon," I said.

"Elvirey!"

"I reckon, *ma'am*," I said.

There wasn't much to do. A pot of beans had stewed all day. The corn bread was ready baked.

"You can set the table," the widow said. "Use those willow pattern plates."

They was nice, them plates. Nicer than any my mam ever had. I wished I had the grit to drop one!

Whilst I set out the plates and the spoons, I took a long look at her cabin. A bright pieced quilt spread up her bed. There was curtains at the window. On the wall hung a feed-store calendar and a pencil sketch of a man.

"My late husband," the widow said. "I miss him."

"My mam had pictures on the wall." I hadn't meant to say it.

"Did she now?" said the widow. "And books? Did your mother read, like me?"

"How did *you* know?" I said. I could see her books on a shelf by the hearth.

"I wish I had known her," the widow said. "I'm right sorry she passed, Elvira."

"Yes, ma'am," I said.

Chapter 6

Indian Pudding

On the last day, we worked 'til candlelight. The Aiken corn was 'most cribbed.

"Lem and Tobe and I can do the rest," the widow said at last. "Come on in to supper."

"We'll be in," said Pap, "ready for supper when it's ready for us."

"Then Elvira and I will go ready it," said Widow Aiken.

But when the table was set and the food laid on, Pap and them still hadn't come.

Widow Aiken lit the lamp and sank into her

chair. She heaved a sigh and closed her eyes, weary-like.

I crept to the shelf to take a look at them books.

"Would you like to borrow one, Elvira?" Her voice made me jump.

"Sis can read," I muttered, hanging my head. "Bub too, real good. Mam learned *them*, but . . ."

Just then they all came in, Pap and Sis and Tobe and Lem. I ran for the washing-up water.

As we left that night, Widow Aiken put her hand on Pap's arm. "I wish there were some way to thank you," she said.

"I thank you, ma'am," said Pap, his voice all mannerly. "You and me, we make a good team."

I stopped my ears and ran down the trail as far as I could see by the light of her open door.

That's that, I thought. That's the last we need to have any truck with the Widow Aiken.

For a week or more, we was busy on our own place. Bub's knee got right enough for him to work with Pap. Sis and me helped Granny put up our winter stores.

Then, on a Sabbath day, there she was at our door with her boys, an Indian pudding in her hands.

"I'd be obliged if you'd help me with my quilt," said Granny when they'd made their howdy-do's. "Quiltin's a lonesome thing without company."

Quicker than two shakes of a lamb's tail, the boys had Granny's quilting frame set up in front of the cabin. Granny and the widow woman sat in the sun, jawing like they hadn't visited in a month of Sundays.

"Want to join us, girls?" the Widow Aiken said.

Sis pulled a stool close, but I shook my head.

"I have somethin' to do," I said.

I clumb up Bub's tree to watch. The boys took off to the woods to hunt squirrel, but Pap didn't go. He hung around, making this excuse or that to stay near. He looked so moony, it made me sick.

I didn't come outen that tree 'til she was gone, though they called and called at supper time.

When I did finally go in, they had et up the Indian pudding!

Chapter 7

ABCs

Next thing you know, we're threshing the wheat together, the Aikens and us, and then we're all husking corn. Pap's traipsing over to help the widow build fence. She's at our cabin putting up sauerkraut.

Before I knowed it, the widow was at our place 'most every Monday, helping with the wash. Got so's a path was beaten from her door to our'n. Sis was at her cabin so much I began to wonder just where Sis lived!

Not me. When the widow came into our

cabin, I went out. When some of my folks fetched over to her place, I was busy to home.

"Elvira," I heard her say once or twice, her voice all soft and sweet.

I played like I didn't hear.

Then the widow brought a book with her. She put it down, casual-like, on a stool beside the hearth. She set about baking with Granny and Sis, mixing and kneading and shaping the loaves. Granny set me to fetch water from the spring, and I bided outside when my chore was done. But the wind came up. It nipped my ears.

In time, I went inside. Granny was setting a pie into the Dutch oven, and the bread was on the hearth to rise.

I sidled to the stool while they was busy at the table. The book's leather cover looked soft to touch. But I didn't touch, only looked.

"Would you like to hear a story while the bread's rising?"

How did that woman know every time I gawked at a book?

I shook my head. But Sis was crying, "Oh, yes, ma'am. That would surely be a treat!"

I got busy away from the fire with my corncob doll. She was called Caroline, after Mam.

"We'll just pay them no mind, Caroline," I whispered.

Only Caroline *would* listen. I nursed her in my arms and sang to her loud as I dared, but pretty soon she was listening to the queer goings on of a midsummer's night and a fellow name of Bottom.

The widow didn't seem to notice when we crept near.

Next time she came to our cabin, she called out to me as she walked through the door.

"Elvira, I have something for you," she said.

"Don't want it," I said right back.

But Granny shot me a look that curled my hair.

My hand reached out for what the widow put in it. A slate pencil and a slate, with something written on it—*ABC*.

"You might copy those letters," the widow said. "You might practice saying their sounds— ay or ah, buh, and kuh or suh. If you like, next time I'll teach you more."

"That's right kindly of you, missus," Granny said. "What do you say, Elvirey?"

I looked at the floor.

"What do you *say*, Elvirey?"

A body *had* to speak up when Granny used that voice.

"Thank you," I said.

But the widow turned away. She and Granny commenced stringing berries to dry. They paid no mind to me.

Chapter 8

Wildflower Crown

Mam was gonna learn me reading. She had learned Sis, though Pap called it foolishness, Sis being a gal and all. But before Mam had a chance, she was sick. And then she was gone.

When I asked to learn my letters, Sis was busy with Mam's work. And Granny . . . well, Granny could parse out her Bible, a verse at a time, but . . .

I stayed ignorant.

Then the Widow Aiken said, "I'll teach you." So I studied her *A*, *B*, and *C*, until I knew them by heart. I found other letters in Granny's Bible and copied them on my slate. I wondered what sounds they made.

And time went by. Tobe and Lem and Bub hunted, and we shared out the meat. The widow and Granny and Sis sewed and baked and washed. Sometimes, of an evening, the Aikens gathered at our cabin, and the widow read aloud. Then Pap walked her home, though her boys was right by.

She said nary a word more to me.

'Til I purely couldn't stand it!

"I know *ABC*," I said one quilting day. "What about the rest? You promised you would learn me!"

"Elvirey, mind your manners," Granny said. She didn't look up from her needle.

The widow kept placing her stitches, small and even and slow.

I rubbed my toe on my heel. I felt myself falling in the silence, so deep between us two.

"Please," I whispered. "Please learn me."

"I said I would teach you, Elvira," the widow said, " . . . *if* you liked."

My learning commenced that day. D, E, F, G, H, I. When I could write all my letters and tell all their sounds, the widow smiled proud-like and gave me a hug.

The snow was thick on the ground. By the fire, I studied over the words in her books and practiced on my slate. One day, I wrote my name . . . then Pap's and Granny's and Sis's and Bub's. I read a word, then two . . . then a whole verse of Granny's Bible. Then a page! And I copied it out.

While I read and wrote, Widow Aiken stitched on a dress for me, a dress of my own, not handed down from Sis! I had to admit it was pretty, as pretty as Mam ever made. I thought she'd be glad for me iffen she knowed.

I didn't need Granny to put me in mind to say, "Thank you."

In the spring, we had the wedding at the widow's cabin. All the neighbors came. There was a preacher from the new township. Tobe gave the bride away.

I wore my new dress. Sis wore hers, too, that she'd sewed with the widow's help.

Sis wove a wreath for the widow's hair. A wreath of wildflowers like Mam had loved. The widow wore it as she and Pap said their vows.

Then Granny brought out her Bible. She smiled at the widow, and the widow smiled at me.

"Will you set down our marriage, Elvira, in the Good Book?"

"Oh, no, Widow Aiken," I said.

"Not a widow no more," Pap said, his face all a-beam.

"Hannah," the widow said. "Call me Hannah, Elvira."

She put the pen in my hand.

"Please," she whispered.

So I set it down, though my hand trembled and I made a blotch or two. And all our neighbors watched.

Clayton W. Freshwater and Hannah M. Aiken
Sixth of May, 1833

Hannah lifted the wreath from off her head and set it down on mine.

"A crown for Elvira," she said.

"Tarnation, that's right," Pap cried with a laugh. "All this was Elvirey's idee!"

J
Fiction Howard
Howard, Ellen.
Log cabin wedding /

1/07